The Queen Is Coming to Tea

To my parents, the King and Queen of my heart
—LRL

For Lua
—CVK

Cover and internal design © 2017 by Sourcebooks, Inc.
Text © 2017 by Linda Ravin Lodding
Cover and internal illustrations © Constanze von Kitzing

Sourcebooks and the colophon are registered trademarks of Sourcebooks, Inc.

Acrylic paint and color pencils were used to prepare the full color art.

Published by Sourcebooks Jabberwocky, an imprint of Sourcebooks, Inc.
P.O. Box 4410, Naperville, Illinois 60567-4410
(630) 961-3900
Fax: (630) 961-2168
www.jabberwockykids.com

Library of Congress Cataloging-in-Publication data is on file with the publisher.

Source of Production: Leo Paper, Heshan City, Guangdong Province, China
Date of Production: October 2016
Run Number: 5007703

Printed and bound in China.
LEO 10 9 8 7 6 5 4 3 2 1

The Queen Is Coming to Tea

Linda Ravin Lodding

Constanze von Kitzing

 sourcebooks
jabberwocky

One day, there was a knock at Ellie's door.

There stood the Queen's Footman.

"A message from Her Royal Highness."

He offered Ellie a note on a silver tray.

MAY I PLEASE
COME FOR TEA?

SINCERELY YOURS,
THE QUEEN
HERSELF

"We'd be honored!" said Ellie. She turned to her elephant. "But we don't have much time to prepare, do we, Langley?"

Langley didn't seem concerned.

"Pish posh," Ellie said. "We can do it."
She turned to the Footman. "The Queen is welcome to tea," she said. "But I must get cake."

"Splendiferous idea," said the Footman. "The Queen does love cake."

Straight away,
Ellie grabbed Langley
and hopped on a plane
to Paris.

They skipped past the Eiffel Tower to
La Patisserie.

"Chef whips up the best cream-filled cakes
in the world," Ellie told Langley.

"Très delicious!" agreed Chef.

And home they flew with the cake and Chef,
who wanted to meet the Queen.

A little while later, the Queen's Footman
knocked again.

"When, Mademoiselle, will tea be served?"

"Soon," said Ellie. "I must hurry and get the tea."

"Grand," said the Footman. "The Queen does love tea."

So, Ellie and Langley hopped
onto a rickshaw and high-tailed
it to China to visit
Ming.

"Ming makes the best tea," she told Langley. "The tea leaves are shaped like a dragon's tongue."

"Best tea," agreed Ming.

And home they went with the tea and Ming, who wanted to meet the Queen.

They hadn't been home but a moment when the Queen's Footman arrived. "When will tea be served, Mademoiselle?"

"Soon," said Ellie. "I must get lemons for her tea."

"Smashing idea!" said the Footman. "The Queen does love lemon with tea."

"I know just the spot," Ellie said to Langley.

When they landed in Italy,
they hired a car and driver.
(Ellie didn't trust Langley
behind the wheel.)

"To the Amalfi Coast! Pronto!" Ellie instructed Luigi,
her driver. Once there, they plucked a bushel of lovely *limoni*.

"That's the Italian word for lemons," she told Langley.

Langley said he knew this already.

And home they went with the lemons and Luigi, who
wanted to meet the Queen.

Moments after they arrived home, there was a
tap! tap! tap! on the door.

"Good day," said the Queen's Footman.

And before the Footman could ask, Ellie said, "Soon.
But I can't wear these clothes to tea with the Queen. I must
have a fancy dress."

"Of course!" said the Footman. "The Queen wouldn't
have it any other way."

Ellie and Langley hailed a taxi
to New York City and marched into
Miss Twinkle's dressing rooms
at the ballet.

"Excuse me, Miss Twinkle," (she was the prima ballerina and an old friend of Ellie's) "might I borrow your fluffiest, fanciest, frilliest tutu?"

Miss Twinkle presented Ellie with her most glamorous tutus.

Ellie and Miss Twinkle pirouetted all the way home to meet the Queen. (Langley took a taxi. He wasn't so light on his toes.)

The trio got back just in time to
meet the Queen's Footman.
"When—?" he asked.

"Tea will be served at two o'clock," said Ellie.

Ellie and her friends set the table with flowers and the finest china. They hung ribbons around Ellie's bedroom. They set out the cake, the teapot, and the lemons. And waited for two o'clock.

While they waited, they ate just a little piece of cake. And drank just a little tea. And Langley ate just one lemon. (Too many and he gets a sour tummy.)

Then they started to play and dance, giggle and prance.

Before Ellie realized it, they had eaten nearly all the cake. Drank nearly all the tea. And they were so tired from playing and dancing, giggling and prancing, they all fell sound asleep.

No one heard the doorbell ring.

No one, except Ellie.

Ellie and the Queen had tea for two.

And they both loved that.

The next morning, Ellie saw a note on her door.

May I come today for a feast?
Sincerely yours,
The King
Himself

Straight away,
Ellie grabbed Langley
and hopped on a plane
to Paris.